The Fool of the WORLD and the Flying Ship

A Ukrainian Folk Tale

Adapted and Illustrated by Valeri Gorbachev

STAR BRIGHT BOOKS

NEW YORK

Library of Congress Cataloging-in-Publication Data:

Gorbachev, Valeri.
    Fool of the world and the flying ship / by Valeri Gorbachev.
32p.   31.5 x 21.5 cm
Summary: When the Czar proclaims that he will marry his daughter
to the man who brings him a flying ship, the Fool of the World sets
out to try his luck and meets some unusual companions on the way.
    ISBN: 1-887734-19-8 (hardcover)
    [1. Folklore--Ukraine.]   I. Title
PZ8.1.G6367Fo 1997
[398.2 ' 09477 ' 02]--dc21   96-30082
                                                    C I P
                                                    AC

ISBN :1-887734-19-8

For Deborah Shine

Once upon a time, the Tsar sent his messengers to every town and village in the land. They carried an extraordinary proclamation:

The Tsar desires a flying ship.
Whoever brings one to him shall
marry his daughter, the Tsarevna.

No one had ever seen a flying ship. It seemed impossible that such a thing could exist. But in one village, there lived a quiet young man whom everyone called the Fool of the World. He announced that he would go at once and find such a ship. Everyone laughed at him, but he decided to go anyway. His mother packed bread and water for his journey, he thanked her graciously, and set off.

He had not gone far when he met an old man.
"Where are you going?" asked the man.

"To find a flying ship," he replied.

"Where will you find such a ship?"

"I don't know, yet," said the Fool.

"Well, other men have passed this way in search of a flying ship, but you are the first to stop and talk, so I will help you. But before anything else, let us eat. Open your bag."

"Alas, I have little to share," said the Fool. "But you are welcome to whatever there is."

"Look in your bag," said the old man. When the Fool opened his bag, he gasped. It was filled with delicious food.

After they had eaten, the old man said,
"Go to the woods and strike the first tree
you come to three times. You will then fall
asleep. When you awake you will find
your flying ship."

The Fool thanked the old man and set off.
When he got to the woods, he did as he had
been instructed. He struck the first tree three
times, and soon fell asleep.

When he awoke, he could hardly
believe his eyes. There beside him, floating
just above the ground, was a ship. He
immediately climbed aboard, and it rose
slowly into the sky.

Silently the ship moved through the air. Before long the Fool saw a man kneeling in the road with his ear pressed to the ground.

"What are you doing?" he called.

"I am listening to everything that is said in the world," the man replied.

"Come with me to visit the Tsar," said the Fool. "You are sure to hear much that is interesting at the palace."

"I can hear it all from here," said Hear-all. "But I will come anyway. I would like to see the palace." And he climbed aboard the flying ship.

The Fool and Hear-all flew on and soon they saw a man hopping on one leg.

"Why are you hopping on one leg?" they called.

"Because if I used two legs I would be across the world in one step."

"Then you must be very fast," said the Fool. "Perhaps the Tsar could use you as his messenger. Come with us to visit him."

"So I will," replied Stride-far and he climbed aboard.

The three men flew on. Eventually they saw a man with a bow and arrow. They all looked and looked but could not see what he was aiming at.

"Hello!" called the Fool. "What are you aiming at?"

"I am aiming at a target a hundred miles away," replied the man.

"You must have very sharp eyes!" said the Fool. "Come with us. We are taking this flying ship to the Tsar, and I am going to marry the Tsarevna. The Tsar could use someone with eyes such as yours to keep watch over his kingdom."

So Sharp-eyes climbed aboard the ship, and the men sailed on.

After a while they saw a fellow with an enormous sack of bread. They all felt hungry, so they called down to him.

"May we have some of your bread?"

"Sorry, this bread is for my dinner."

"But you have a whole sackful."

"What, this load? This is but one mouthful for me," replied the man.

"We are going to see the Tsar," called the Fool. "There you will find plenty of bread. Come with us."

So Hungry-eater climbed aboard, and they continued on their way.

The travelers saw a man in a lake. "What are you doing?" the Fool called.

"I am looking for something to drink."

"But you are in a lake!" said the Fool.

"Ah, this is but a sip for me," said Thirsty-drinker.

"Come with us to visit the Tsar. You are sure to find enough to drink at the palace."

So Thirsty-drinker climbed aboard.

Next, the men in the ship saw a man carrying a large bundle of wood into a forest.

"Why are you carrying wood *into* the forest?" the Fool called. "It is usual to come *out* of a forest carrying wood."

"This is magic wood," replied the man. "If I scatter it in a forest, an army of soldiers will spring up."

"Bring your wood and come with us, for we are on our way to the palace."

So Wood-carrier climbed aboard, and once more the ship flew on.

The Fool saw a man carrying an enormous
bundle of straw.

"Where are you going with all that straw?"
he called down.

"Ah, this is special straw," said Straw-carrier.
"Wherever I scatter this straw, snow will fall and
frost will set in."

"I am sure that will be useful to the Tsar," said
the Fool. "Come with us to visit him."

So Straw-carrier climbed aboard, and on they
flew.

At last the travelers came to the palace.
From his window, the Tsar saw the ship.
At once he sent a servant to inquire which
prince had arrived.

"Alas," his servant reported. "There is no prince. There is only a foolish peasant and his companions."

The Tsar was worried. He had said that whoever brought him a flying ship could marry his daughter.

He did not think anyone but a prince would succeed. Now here was a foolish peasant with a flying ship. He could not imagine his daughter marrying a poor peasant, yet he could not escape his promise.

The Tsar decided to set the Fool an impossible task. "Tell the peasant to bring me a jar of water from the Well of Happiness, on the other side of the world. And tell him to bring it before dinnertime," he told his servant.

Hear-all told the Fool what the Tsar was saying.

"I could not reach the palace gate before dinnertime," lamented the Fool. "So how can I do that?"

"*Ha!*" said Stride-far. "That is just a step away." And with one great stride he disappeared. At the Well of Happiness, Stride-far filled a jar with the magic water and then he sat down and fell asleep.

The Fool anxiously waited for Stride-far. Soon the
Tsar would sit down to dinner. Hear-all pressed his ear
to the ground. "I can hear Stride-far snoring," he said.

"What shall we do?" asked the Fool.

"I will take care of that," said Sharp-eyes.
He picked up his bow and sent an arrow flying into
the well. The splashing water woke Stride-far, who
jumped up and in one step was back at the palace.

The Tsar was very surprised when he saw the water. "I shall set the Fool another task," he decided.

To his servant he said, "Tell the peasant that I need to be sure he has an appetite fit for the son-in-law of a tsar. He and his companions must eat twenty roasted oxen and forty ovens full of bread."

"What now?" the Fool lamented. "That is impossible!"

But Hungry-eater smacked his lips and said, "Ah, food at last. I thought they would never feed us."

So Hungry-eater ate most of the food, barely leaving any for his companions. "A mere morsel," he complained. "You would think that one could get a decent meal at the Tsar's palace."

"I will beat the Fool yet," the Tsar said to himself.

To his servant he said, "Tell the Fool that if he wishes to marry the Tsarevna he must drink forty barrels of wine."

"What next?" cried the Fool. "I can hardly drink one tumbler of wine. How shall I manage forty barrels?"

But Thirsty-drinker said, "At last! I have been waiting for something to drink for hours."

"Send the wine," the Fool told the Tsar's servant. When it arrived, Thirsty-drinker said, "What meager portions the Tsar gives," and he swallowed the lot.

The Tsar was furious, so he made yet another plan.

"Tell the Fool he must bathe before he marries the Tsarevna," he instructed his servant. Then he commanded that when the Fool was inside the bathhouse, it was to be made so hot that he would burn up.

But the Fool and Straw-carrier had already made a plan. As soon as the bathhouse door was locked behind them, Straw-carrier scattered his straw, and snow began to fall. There was scarcely time to wash before frost covered everything.

When the door was unlocked in the morning, the Fool said, "Thank you, it was beginning to get chilly in here."

By now, the Tsar was nearly exploding with anger.
He called his servant. "Tell the Fool that he must come to
the wedding at the head of a great army, or there will be
no marriage." The Tsar was sure he would be rid of the
peasant now.

Hear-all told the Fool what the Tsar was saying.

"What shall I do?" cried the Fool, "All of
you have helped me outwit the Tsar, but
now I fear our luck
has run out."

"Have you forgotten me?" asked Wood-carrier.
"You will have an army in the morning. "Tell the
Tsar that if he does not keep his word, you will
conquer him and take his kingdom."

That night Wood-carrier scattered his sticks.
Where each one landed, a soldier sprang up and
instantly fell into line.

In the morning, the Tsar saw a great army.
At once, he sent out gifts of jewels and silk,
and welcomed the Fool.

In his smart silk robes the Fool looked splendid. He had learned much from the kindness of his companions and soon came to be a very wise man. The Tsarevna thought he was handsome and clever, and they had a joyous wedding.

The Tsar grew very fond of the Fool, and gave him, and each of his companions, an important place in court.